QUAKE!

By Mike Graf

Illustrated by Samuel Sakaria

Pearson Australia
(a division of Pearson Australia Group Pty Ltd)
20 Thackray Road, Port Melbourne, Victoria 3207
PO Box 460, Port Melbourne, Victoria 3207
www.pearson.com.au

Sydney, Melbourne, Brisbane, Perth, Adelaide
and associated companies around the world

Publisher: Simone Calderwood
Illustrator: Samuel Sakaria
Editor: Fiona Cooke
Designer: Glen McClay
Copyright & Pictures Editor: Helen Mammides
Project Editor: Aisling Coughlan
Production Controller: Claire Henry
Printed in Malaysia (CTP-VVP)

ISBN 978 1 4425 2809 3

Pearson Australia Group Pty Ltd   ABN 40 004 245 943

CONTENTS

CHAPTER 1

POOCH

This is my story, all here in my journal for safekeeping. I can hardly believe these things happened to me! It all started on a bright, sunny day...

I left school and headed towards the city along West Street, my usual route home. This gets me to Mum's office, and she drives us the rest of the way home once she has finished work.

On the day I am writing about, I noticed how the sun glared off the tall buildings along the street. The nine-storey Union Bank Building where my mum works looked tall and imposing.

I glanced towards the sixth floor, where Mum has her office. I would be up there soon, but there was somewhere else I wanted to stop first.

Near the corner of West Street and Federation Avenue is my favourite milk bar. I walked up a few steps and opened the door to the shop. Mr Alexander was at the cash register and Mrs Alexander was restocking shelves with tins of soup from an open box.

They both looked up and smiled as I came in. I smiled back, then headed down the aisle to get myself a bottle of water, a banana and a packet of crackers.

Just as I turned out of the aisle, heading towards the register, a large tan labrador jumped out at me. I fell backwards against a shelf, bringing down some tins with me.

The dog leaned over me and licked my face.

Mr Alexander hurried over. "Sorry, sorry, sorry," he called out, yanking the labrador away.

I straightened up and reached out to pat the dog's head. "It's okay. I like dogs," I said.

Mr Alexander said, "It's the third time he's done this today."

"How come he has so much energy?"

"He's just a puppy. I don't think he's completely trained."

"He was left by the door of our shop yesterday morning," Mrs Alexander chipped in. "We have signs up, but so far no-one's claimed him. I think he might have been abandoned."

I looked at the nearly full-grown puppy, trying to imagine what could have happened to him. Then I reached down to pat his head again. He jumped onto me, his tail wagging crazily.

"He likes you," Mr Alexander said, smiling.

"I can see that," I replied, bracing myself against another tumble into the shelves.

Mr Alexander glanced towards his wife and then back at me. "Perhaps you can do us a favour while he's here. My wife and I can't leave the shop when it's open. Would you mind taking him for a walk, at least while we have him? He's a puppy, and he really needs more than we can offer."

I thought this over for a second, then answered. "Yeah, I think so. But I have to ask my mum first. I'm on my way to her office now. By the way, what's his name?"

"We don't know, so for the time being we're calling him Pooch."

Mr Alexander and I smiled, knowing that wasn't very original.

I paid for my food, hugged the puppy and stepped outside. By then, the tall buildings were in partial shade. The sun had begun slipping down the late-afternoon sky.

CHAPTER 2

MY FAVOURITE PUPPY

After school the next day, I poked my head into the Alexanders' shop.

"Is my favourite puppy in here?" I called out.

Mrs Alexander looked up, saw me, and smiled.

"We have him out the back," she told me. "He knocked down some food again and jumped on another customer. It was getting ridiculous."

Mrs Alexander led me to the back of the shop. I smiled and waved to Mr Alexander, who was scanning groceries at the register. We opened the back door and there was Pooch, tied to a pole in the alley. He saw me and leapt forward, his tail wagging at full speed.

I walked over to him and he jumped up, licking my face.

"My mum said I can take him to the park for half an hour," I said to Mrs Alexander. "After that, I have to meet her at work."

"That's great," said Mrs Alexander, relieved. "He really needs to run off some of his energy."

Together, Mrs Alexander and I untied Pooch from the pole. Immediately, he began lunging back through the shop, leading me towards the front door. I gripped the lead firmly as he pulled.

"He's strong!" I announced, as I was tugged forward, sliding, across the shop's slick floor.

"Here, wait," Mr Alexander called out.

I pulled back on the lead to stop Pooch from dragging me out the door.

Mr Alexander hurried over to me. "Take some of these," he said.

The shopkeeper handed me several dog biscuits. I pocketed them, then headed towards the front door.

"See you in thirty minutes," I called over my shoulder, as Pooch and I stepped outside.

I tried to lead Pooch towards the park. Instead, he guided me to unexpected places. Around the corner was one of those spots. He was yanking me towards an empty car park. As we headed towards it, I noticed a pile of broken bricks and cement near the back. I tugged on the lead, trying to re-route my canine companion.

"Hey, Pooch," I called out, tugging against the straining lead. "Hey! I don't even know your real name."

But as much as I tried, I couldn't sway Pooch from his preferred destination. His senses led him right towards the rubble, sniffing enthusiastically—but there didn't seem to be anything there but rubbish.

Finally, I had to yank him back forcefully. "Okay, that's enough of that."

This time, Pooch obeyed me. I gave him a biscuit as a reward. Together we walked out of the car park.

We barely had enough time to circle the park before I noticed it was 4:30. We hurried back, passing Mum's building along the way.

When we got to the shop, I saw a sign posted in the window to the right of the entrance:

**Lost dog.
Tan labrador. Very friendly.
Staying at shop.
Please inquire within.**

I patted Pooch's head and he licked me again.

"Someone's very lucky to have you as a pet," I said. Then I took the dog inside.

"I hope you find his owner!" I said, as I handed the lead to Mr Alexander.

"We do, too," Mrs Alexander replied.

Then she came over and handed me a bag.

"This is for you," she said warmly.

"Thanks," I replied. I stuffed the bag into my pack and opened the door.

"Can you come back again tomorrow?" Mrs Alexander asked.

"Sure. Mum said I could walk him the rest of the week."

CHAPTER 3

CHAOS ALL OVER

The next day, we circled the park again. I worked up a sweat, trying to keep up with the energetic puppy.

We were on our way back, when suddenly Pooch started yelping and barking like crazy.

Pooch had barked at things before, but this was different. He was in a frenzy.

I remember my body tensing as Pooch continued to bark and bark. I looked around, but I couldn't see anything unusual.

15

Then Pooch went quiet. He lay down and began to snarl. It was eerie watching him and my skin tingled.

That's when the ground started shaking. I stood still, holding onto Pooch's lead. Down the avenue, I could see buildings swaying. A street light was rocking back and forth as if it was really windy.

An earthquake!

As the ground continued to shake, I grabbed a stop sign, bracing myself. I looked around and saw some people standing still. Others were running with panicked looks on their faces. They blinked into the sun, trying to work out what kind of danger they were in.

As quickly as the earthquake had started, it stopped. Within seconds, the pulse of the city seemed to return to what it had been before.

Pooch sat up normally as if nothing had happened. I reached down and patted his head, then gave him a biscuit. The two of us continued our walk back to the shop.

We got there within a few minutes. As soon as we stepped inside, I noticed tins, bottles and packages of food strewn across the floor, many smashed open. One of the shelves had fallen against another.

"This isn't your fault!" I said to my companion.

The mess on the floor wasn't the only thing that was wrong. It was dark, and the ceiling fans were off. There was no-one around. A siren wailed somewhere in the distance.

"Mr Alexander. Mrs Alexander!" I called out. "Hello. Is anyone here?"

I poked my head down a few aisles. All I saw was more mess.

Suddenly, the ground thrust upwards. It was a huge jolt this time. I saw shelves lurch forward and tumble to the ground. Then the whole shop started shaking. It felt as though there was a giant beast outside, rattling the building. Several of the shop windows crashed out. Outside, I heard people screaming.

Pooch lurched towards the entrance and instinctively I followed. We made it to the front door, dodging falling food and shelves along the way. I remember stepping into a pile of spilt sugar and having to shake it off with my foot.

I balanced against the door frame while I struggled to get the door open. The roof of the building began to buckle. I saw wood splintering and cracking above my eyes, and the ceiling began caving in.

Which way to go? It seemed safer outside, but I knew that during an earthquake, it was better to stay inside, if that's where I was when the quake started.

Pooch had been growling and snarling the whole time, but at least he was still with me.

As I hesitated, I was knocked down by something falling from above. My head rang. I crawled the rest of the way down the stairs, hardly knowing what I was doing.

People were screaming and running in random directions. It looked like the time I had stirred up an ant pile and watched the little insects scurrying in a frenzy all over the place. Now, the people were the insects.

Just then, a street pole collapsed onto a car, smashing the windshield. And now the ground was rolling in waves beneath me. This long, mesmerising moment made me feel as though I had been hypnotised.

I had always lived in this city, so I had experienced earthquakes before—but nothing like this one.

I crouched at the bottom of the steps, trembling, and for a few seconds I watched the chaos all around me—windows breaking, cars crashing, street lights toppling to the ground, a policeman blowing his whistle, buildings swaying, chunks of brick and cement falling all over the place and smashing into bits of rubble.

I needed to get back inside. I crawled slowly back up the steps and through the door.

I was looking up, checking for danger, just as a giant beam began to collapse. I lunged away and the large, splintered piece of wood just missed me. It crashed right across the lead binding Pooch and me together, instantly snapping the leather rope in half.

"Hey!" I yelled, as Pooch took off.

Then, in a moment I'll never forget, the building began to close in on me. Wood, glass, food, shelves and ceiling tiles showered down. Another large beam knocked against my right arm, hurling me to the ground.

I screamed as things continued to pummel me from all over. Something smashed against my leg. Another object grazed my head. I tucked myself into a ball and huddled, trying to protect my head and face, waiting for the whole thing to just stop.

More debris pounded down, but I realised I wasn't being hit directly any more. Maybe a minute of this went by, or was it a few minutes or more? It felt like forever, and as if the whole world was piling on top of me.

Eventually the uproar ended and it grew quiet. I coughed several times, tilted my head and passed out.

CHAPTER 4

BURIED ALIVE

The next few minutes—or was it hours?
—were like a bad dream.

At first I wasn't even sure I was alive.
At some point, though, I regained full
consciousness. Even then, things didn't
seem real.

I knew I was buried. All kinds of things were
above and around me. There were shattered
pieces of wood, bricks, broken glass, computer
parts, dust and who knows what else.

A piece of splintered board, with a nail sticking out of it, was aimed right at my head. I pushed it away, but then things shifted above. My body tensed, sensing more doom, but nothing else crashed down.

Slowly, I removed what was on top of me. As I did, I realised I couldn't move my right arm without cringing. It hurt to breathe.

And the dust—I could taste it in my mouth. Using my good arm, I brushed off as much of it as I could while spitting out the gunk. I wished I had something to breathe through. I just kept inhaling more of the stuff.

I tried to shift to a more comfortable position. It didn't work well and I realised that I was pretty much stuck where I was. I could lift my head a little, but that made me feel dizzy.

I can't get out of here! I realised. My heart began to race. It felt as though I was having a heart attack. My breathing was totally out of control.

Do I have asthma now? I thought. I was freaking out.

The taste of blood snapped me out of my panic. It was trickling down my face and into my mouth. It was warm and tasted of salt blended with the chalkiness of dust.

I tried to lift my injured arm to check my wound. From the intense pain, I realised I probably had a broken arm and that I should not move it. I attempted to flex my hand a few times into a fisted ball, but the pain was too much to bear and I stopped.

I shifted my focus to other parts of my body. I could wiggle my toes and my legs felt okay. I had some pain in my chest, but it didn't seem too bad.

All the while, though, it felt as though something was wedged into my back. I tried shifting my weight to relieve the pressure, but some more debris showered down. I gently brushed it off and realised again what a terrible predicament I was in. I had to try to stay calm and still.

That's when I heard panicked, distressed voices calling out. People were shouting for help, screaming and moaning. There were rescuers finding bodies, and sirens all around. I could even hear the *WHOCK* ... *WHOCK* ... *WHOCK* of a helicopter. But it all seemed so far away.

Then I heard someone shout, "Is anyone down there?"

I was about to answer, when someone else yelled, "I think I broke my leg!"

I tried to figure out where I might be in all the turmoil, but my head was at an angle and I couldn't get a decent view. So I listened some more.

"Have you seen my wife?" a man's voice pleaded. "Has anyone seen my wife? Where is my wife?"

I realised it was Mr Alexander. I gulped, wanting to help him.

"Does anyone know where my wife is?" he tried again.

It was obvious he was in shock.

"Sir!" a strong voice commanded.

"Sir, we need to get you out of here. It's too dangerous here."

"But my wife!" Mr Alexander begged, before his voice faded away.

I continued to listen until a new sound struck me like a dagger. A dog was whimpering somewhere.

CHAPTER 5

AN UNDERGROUND REUNION

The whimpering continued. I was sure it was Pooch, but I was unable to twist my body or head enough to look for him. I didn't know if he could see me.

Then, moving very slowly, I managed to lift my body just a little, and turn my head slowly here and there. Then the pain gripped me again and I had to lie flat.

There was another whimper.

"Here, Pooch," I called out. "I'm here, boy!"

The dog's cries grew more urgent. Soon I heard a small "Ruff, ruff."

Pooch had heard me!

"Here, boy," I called again, this time more hopeful.

I heard movement. Pooch was wriggling along and the sounds were getting louder.

"Good boy!" I encouraged him. "Good boy! Come on, keep coming."

I really can't tell you how Pooch finally got to me, but at last I could smell his breath and the sounds were right there, next to me.

"Yeah, Pooch, you made it!"

Pooch nudged his face into my chest and immediately started licking me.

"Ahhh!" I flinched in pain—but I was smiling.

Pooch couldn't contain his enthusiasm. He kept on licking!

Somehow we managed to adjust. I patted my stomach and coaxed him to lie down next to me, with his head resting on my lap.

It seemed as though we were both crying. I know I was, anyway. We huddled like long-lost war buddies.

I continued stroking Pooch's fur. That's when I noticed his breathing was shallow and laboured.

"It's okay, boy," I said several times, hoping to comfort him.

I saw that both of Pooch's front legs were disfigured and bleeding. He whimpered several times and licked at them profusely. It had to be painful.

I tuned in again to the commotion above. It sounded like all kinds of things were being moved around up there and I heard rescuers calling out.

Most of the time I couldn't tell what was being said. I began to realise, though, that several buildings must have collapsed and that I was quite likely buried under several storeys of debris.

Pooch heard the din, too. In between bouts of licking and whimpering, he perked up his ears, sometimes letting out a small bark.

This continued for what seemed like hours. From time to time, the puppy and I would try to reach the world above.

"Help! We're down here!" I would scream. Pooch would add his barks.

Throughout this time, dust and debris kept drifting down. I was covered with it and it went into my nose and mouth with each breath.

I kept spitting out gunk, until I realised how parched I was. I couldn't get that out of my mind. Dry mouth. Dust. Spit. Cough.

Soon I had nothing left to spit. I could hardly swallow.

I got thirstier and thirstier, while ironically sweat trickled down my back. Pooch was clearly in the same situation. After a bout of whining and barking, he lay his head on my lap, with his tongue hanging out.

I patted him, trying to reassure both of us. "It's okay," I said again. "We'll get out of here. I hope." I whispered that last part.

And that thing was still poking into my back.

"My pack," I said to myself. I squirmed and gradually twisted a strap off one shoulder. Eventually I moved my body around enough that I could slide the pack over my injured arm. As soon as I got it free, I felt much better.

I shifted the pack to my side and held it in place with my body and my injured arm, using the other hand to unzip the main compartment.

That's when I first realised that I had my journal with me. The exact one this account is written in now. (And the dust on it proves it.)

But there was something else in there I'd forgotten about—the bag the Alexanders had given me the day before!

I pulled it out and it was quite heavy. I opened it eagerly and couldn't believe my luck. Two perfectly sealed water bottles were in there—and an apple, a smashed banana and a crumpled energy bar. I could have hugged the Alexanders right then!

My first thought was to guzzle down the water. I quickly unscrewed the cap, then took one good, long gulp of the best water I've ever tasted. It really was like nectar, even if it did get mixed with the dust in my mouth.

I noticed Pooch was staring at me longingly. I poured some of the water into his mouth. He lapped it up as if he had just arrived at a desert oasis and hadn't had a drink in weeks.

Then I slowed down and screwed the cap back on. We were half done with the first bottle already, I noticed.

I stared up at the mass of debris with renewed hope and strength. I also noticed lights and shadows flickering above. Torches and searchlights, I realised.

"Help!" I screamed—or tried to, with my dust-choked voice. "Help! Down here!"

Then I sealed the water bottle tighter and listened.

CHAPTER 6

HIS NAME IS RUBBLE

Things were being moved around up there. Engines were running—tractors and cranes, and maybe a bulldozer or two, I thought. I pictured a construction crew, hauling away the items that were trapping me.

Every once in a while, I got an idea of what was going on above me from what the rescuers would say to each other. Sometimes it was good news.

"She's alive!" I heard one cry out. (Boy, did that give me hope.)

"Unfortunately, he's dead," I heard another say later, in a sombre voice.

Of course, in between all this, Pooch and I kept calling for help—I, with my raspy voice, and the puppy with his. By now, with all that chaos above, I really didn't have much hope that the people up there would hear us. They seemed such a long way away.

Sometimes, lights from above would flash into our dreary underworld, penetrating our dusty cave.

I have to admit that, at this point, I felt pretty pessimistic. My arm, head and chest ached. More and more, I felt as though I had been buried alive.

At some point, Pooch and I took a break from constantly listening for signs from the world above. I gave him a dog biscuit that I found smashed in my jeans pocket. We also shared the last half of the water bottle, down to the very last drop.

After drinking, Pooch lifted his back leg and sprayed the debris. It trickled towards me and I had to adjust my position to avoid the little stream. Then there was the smell. I didn't mind too much, until I thought of what would happen if we were rescued. Would they think I did it?

That's about when I realised that I had to go, too. I had no idea of how I would go about it. I'm not a dog, after all. So, for a while, I just ignored my need and focused on trying to stay reasonably comfortable.

Have you ever been deep inside a cave, down one of its dark, narrow passages? Can you imagine how claustrophobic that would feel? I guess that was something like what I was going through, except I had no idea of how or when I would get out. And it was so warm down there. More sweat trickled down my back.

I thought it would help distract me if I could write about what was happening, so I dug around in my bag for my journal and a pen.

I would make some notes with the help of the flickering light from above. It didn't work, though—it was too dark to write.

So I tried to think it all out, imagining how the ordeal would appear in writing. There certainly was plenty of time to think. That's when I remembered my key-ring light.

I carefully sifted through my pack. I was stiff and sore all over and it hurt even more now to move, even a tiny bit. But I found the mini-light and hooked it into one of the straps on my pack.

From that point on, I wrote when I could, using my pack as a desk. It was hard work, with just one good arm, but it was better than doing nothing.

Some piece of equipment—perhaps a tractor?—shifted gears above. This was followed by a period of silence.

Someone called out, "There's a lot of debris below. We'll have to take it away piece by piece, very slowly."

At the sound of people, my wheezing, panting dog lifted his head. His ears perked up. Pooch really wasn't doing that well. I didn't know if it was all the dust getting into his lungs, or if something else was wrong with his chest. The way he treated his paws, I knew they were in bad shape. So for the moment, it was just good to see him respond.

"All that rubble above us is blocking our way out," I said to Pooch.

As I spoke, Pooch wagged his tail and licked my hand.

"Rubble," I repeated.

I now had a real name for Pooch! I also knew that if we ever got out of this, I wanted Rubble to come home with me.

A high-beam light from above started scanning the corridors near us. It was powerful, and it was hard to make out the people around it. I shielded my eyes and gingerly tilted my head upwards. The beam was moving around in random directions, passing near Rubble and me.

Then the light stopped right above me! An instant later, someone frantically shouted, "I found someone!"

The light shifted slightly to Rubble. "And a dog, too."

I looked up and squinted. I knew I was covered in dust, blood and who knows what else. All I could think of at that moment was *Night of the Living Dead*—and I was one of the corpses.

Then the voice screamed exuberantly. "They're alive!"

"Of course we are!" I managed to call out.

"We're going to do what we can to get you out of there as fast as possible," someone called back down.

Hearing that made me breathe a little easier.

CHAPTER 7

A LITTLE CARE PACKAGE

My situation changed quickly after that. It sounded as though several pieces of machinery were being manoeuvred in our direction. That meant we were top priority!

I could picture the crew of rescuers painstakingly removing the shattered debris above us. I imagined a giant game of pick-up-sticks. One by one, they had to take away the pieces without moving anything, in case something fell.

Suddenly, the din stopped. I looked up into the bright light and realised someone was peering down, holding a megaphone.

I had to squint and shield my eyes until the light was shifted slightly. Two firefighters were looking down through the wreckage, right at us!

"Hey," one called into a megaphone. "How are you going?"

My heart pounded. It felt so good to be connected again to the outside world.

"Hi," I shouted as loud as I could, but it hurt to do that. "I'm okay," I lied.

"Are you hurt?"

"Yes."

"Can you move?"

"Not really. I'm trapped and my arm hurts."

"Well, hang in there. It's quite a maze we have to go through to get to you. We don't want to take the chance of anything collapsing. We'll get you out of there as soon as we can."

"Okay," I responded. What else could I say?

The other firefighter held up a canvas bag. "We're sending you a little care package," she called out.

The firefighters looped a rope through the bag's handle. Slowly they began to lower the lifeline towards me.

Right away, it wedged into something. I waited patiently as they worked to free it.

Soon, I heard one of the firefighters announce that the bag was now free. Centimetre by centimetre, I imagined my prize creeping closer—but there were more obstacles lurking. There was more banging and clanging as the bag hit other objects. The firefighters talked to each other. It was as though they were trying to sew the bag through the eye of a needle. Still, I knew the haul was getting close.

I began imagining what was in the bag— books, cake, clothes, food. And water.

Suddenly, I realised the canvas bag was just a metre or two above me.

I looked up and saw it inch down some more. I smelled food, even though what they were sending down probably didn't have much of an aroma! Rubble looked up and weakly wagged his tail.

The bag crept closer. Bits of dust wafted down with it. Then it wedged into something.

The firefighters shook fiercely, but it didn't budge. The bag was just above my head.

"Maybe I can help," I called out.

I reached up, but it was beyond my grasp.

I scanned the area. "Something's got to be around," I said to myself.

I reached for a small splintered stick with my good arm. I grabbed it and poked it upward, jolting the bottom of the bag.

I jostled it again and again.

Then I lifted my body higher and thrust more *oomph* into the bag. It broke free and came crashing down to us.

"Yeah!" I called out.

I immediately turned on my little light, unzipped the bag and inspected the goodies.

I was like a pirate digging into his newly won treasure. But this had to be better! Water bottles, dog biscuits, a muffin, energy bars, fruit, a torch, a first-aid kit and more.

I was rich!

CHAPTER 8

CALL MUM!

For a few wonderful moments, there was a little party in the shattered building on West Street. With my good arm, I turned on the torch. It felt good to see everything around me, but it was also eerie with all the wreckage.

I opened a bottle of water and guzzled half of it.

Rubble stared at me while I did this.

"Don't worry," I said to him between gulps, "your turn is coming!"

I poured the rest of the bottle into Rubble's parched mouth. He lapped up as much as he could.

Next we dived into the food. There were biscuits for Rubble and various goodies for me.

As I devoured the last bit of a blueberry muffin, I realised I had had one like it before— from the Alexanders' bakery! I wondered what that meant.

Then, I realised that the commotion above had come to a halt.

"Hello, down there," someone called down.

I looked up. A rescue worker with a megaphone was gazing right at me.

"Hi," I answered back.

"What's your name?" she asked.

"Jonathon."

"And your dog?"

I looked at the puppy, thinking this would be the first public announcement of his newly chosen title.

"Rubble," I said.

The person above managed a small smile. "Perfect name," she replied.

She held up her hard hat and dust mask. "We'd like you to put these on if you can."

I pulled my own hat and mask out of the bag, put them on, then looked up.

"How long do you think until you can get me out of here?"

The woman sighed, looking at the tangled remains of the building. "It's going to take us a little time. Hang in there. Are you doing okay?"

"My arm and chest hurt, and I'm still a bit dizzy," I replied. "Nothing seems too bad, though. What time is it?"

"Four a.m.," she answered.

"Really?"

"Unless you crawled under the building before the quake, you've been down there nearly twelve hours."

I gulped. "I need to call my mum!"

The woman replied through her megaphone, "Yes, you do! And there is something for that in the bag."

I felt deep inside the bag and found a mobile phone. Then I rang Mum.

CHAPTER 9

ON TV

"Hi, Mum," I announced into the phone.

"Jonathon! I've been so worried. I called everywhere I could think of, then I remembered you were walking the dog. The centre of the city has been closed off. I even tried calling the Alexanders' shop. I couldn't get through. Are you okay?" My mum blurted out all at once.

"Sort of," I replied. "But I'm trapped underneath the building."

"Are you hurt?"

"Yeah. I think I might have a broken my arm. And maybe a few other things," I added, leaving out the details. "I really want to get out of here and go home."

She told me that a news crew above was filming my rescue. While I spoke on the phone, my mum had the television on.

There was a pause in our conversation.

"Wait, Jonathon, I think you're on the news!"

Mum held the phone towards the television set and I heard this announcement:

We've just learned that the boy's name is Jonathon. There's a dog with him. Jonathon is buried beneath what remains of a milk bar on West Street. He has some injuries, but he is conscious and currently in communication with rescuers above. He's been given food and water and the rescue is underway.

The announcement stopped. I noticed a bright light was being aimed towards me.

"Hello, up there!" I yelled towards the light.

There was no response—they must not have heard me. I continued talking to Mum. "Do you know how the Alexanders are?"

"I don't know. I haven't heard anything."

Then my mum saw Rubble on TV. "You've got the dog with you. Is he all right?"

At that point, Rubble's head was in my lap. His breathing was calm for the moment, but shallow.

"I think he's hurt pretty bad," I answered.

"Well, don't move too much. Let the rescuers get you out of there, okay?"

I guess Mum didn't realise, there wasn't much moving I could do!

She started to cry, but this was quickly interrupted by a loud bang.

"What was that?" Mum cried out in alarm.

Rubble lifted his ears and I looked up. A cloud of dust was settling over us. I coughed several times, then realised what was going on.

"They're trying to move some of the wreckage out of the way," I told her.

"I'm on my way down there!" Mum exclaimed.

I hoped they'd let her through to the site.

Minutes passed. The din from the debris removal continued. Then my mobile phone rang. I answered it, and a man asked. "Do you know how to use first aid?"

"Huh?" I replied.

"The first-aid kit," he repeated. "Can you pull it out?"

I grabbed the box from the bag and opened it. Inside were various bandages, pain relief tablets, antiseptic cream and an assortment of other emergency medical supplies. I didn't know quite where to start.

I decided it would be a good idea to start by cleaning the wound on my head. I hung up the phone and slowly, with my good arm, I did what I could. There was a lot of dried blood mixed with dirt. The fiery stinging told me there were cuts here and there I hadn't even been aware of. I cleaned them before smearing on the antiseptic.

I also tried to treat Rubble's paws, but he flinched and growled when I lifted them. I decided that was probably not the best thing to do.

There wasn't much I could do for my bad arm, though. I took two tablets and gulped them down with water.

The longer I was down there, the more stiff and sore I became. It was like being in a tiny cupboard.

I heard the machinery working above me. At times I cringed, afraid something was going to fall down on top of us.

I turned my attention back to the bag. There was something else in there. Its purpose didn't register at first. It was an empty plastic bottle with a lid.

That's when it clicked. It's for going to the toilet—and I *really* had to go.

I glanced up and noticed the light from above beaming down on me. I shouted up, requesting privacy, but no-one seemed to hear.

"Hey!" I yelled again.

This time someone noticed because, a moment later, my phone rang.

"Are you okay?" a voice on the other end asked.

"I've got to go to the toilet," I replied, "and I really don't feel like having the whole world watch."

A moment later, all the lights, cameras and people were directed away. I glanced up one more time, then managed to go...

Boy, was that a relief! I didn't want to be rescued with wet pants.

The phone rang again.

"We're sending a paramedic down," a voice reported.

I looked up and there was a man being lowered in a harness.

CHAPTER 10

MY PERSONAL PARAMEDIC

The paramedic came down slowly, manoeuvring past my now very familiar ceiling decorations.

My observations were interrupted by Rubble's growling. I looked down.

"Are you all right?" I asked, patting his head. But he snarled.

"It's okay, boy," I said, trying to reassure him.

He continued growling—almost as if in warning. Then I got it. He had done the same thing about half a day or so ago.

The ground shook in a succession of jolts.

"Look out!" I heard someone scream.

I looked up. The paramedic was swaying from one wrecked part of the building to another. He grabbed onto a heavy beam and managed to hold himself steady.

As the aftershock continued, debris started raining down again. Something crashed nearby. I curved over to protect myself as best I could, right on top of Rubble. About twenty long seconds later, everything had settled down again.

I slowly peeled myself away from Rubble and gently dusted us off.

Then I looked up and saw that part of the pathway to the world above was now clear. From the way they were gesturing, I could see the rescuers above had noticed this as well.

The paramedic let go of the beam he was holding and started to drop down again, very slowly. A fellow human was getting closer to me!

Soon my personal paramedic looked right down at me.

"Hi!" he said. "My name's Vince."

In just a moment or two, Vince had found a safe spot to stand. Then he called up, "Okay, I'm down."

He went right to work. Using what little space we had, Vince helped me to lie flat. He shone a small light into my pupils.

"They're responding. Good," he announced.

Next, Vince eased off my shoes and touched the bottoms of my feet. "Can you feel that?"

"Yes."

"How does your head feel?"

"I feel a bit woozy and I have a pretty bad headache."

Vince inspected the wound on my head that I had tried to clean earlier. "You've got quite a gash up there. Do you know what did this?"

"It might have been a nail," I said. "But I'm not sure."

"Do you know the last time you had a tetanus injection?" he asked.

I shrugged with the answer. "I don't know."

"We'll deal with that later," Vince said while pulling out a neck brace. "It sounds like your spine is okay, and that's good, but I'm going to put you in this to stabilise your neck just in case. We don't want to take any chances on causing further injury."

Meanwhile, a steel worker had been lowered to a metal beam about halfway between us and the rescue workers above. Now I could finally see what was going on—he was cutting the beam into sections with a heat torch. The different parts were already supported by cables, so they wouldn't fall. I realised that this would clear a pathway to the outside world.

After he put the neck brace on me, the paramedic cleaned my wounds, set my arm in a splint, dressed my head and gave me a more powerful pain tablet. All the attention and treatment made me feel pretty good, as if I was in an underground hospital!

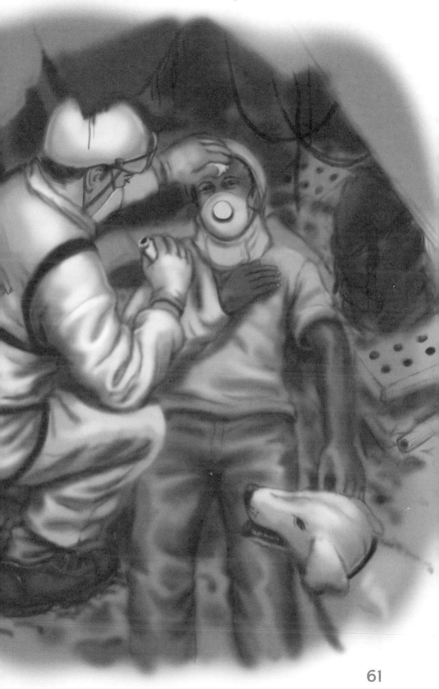

Finally, Vince said, "Now, let's take a look at your friend here."

The doctor gave Rubble a once-over and gently touched his paw.

Rubble woke from his bleary state and viciously snapped at him.

Vince jumped back. "I guess I won't try that again."

"It's okay, Rubble," I said, trying to calm him.

Rubble snapped again, and then growled. Vince moved back a bit.

"Hmmm," Vince said. "Either he doesn't like me or he's really hurting."

"He's hurting," I replied. "He's always been friendly, at least as long as I've known him." I didn't say how long that had been.

Someone above interrupted our discussion. "Should we send a stretcher down now?" they asked through a megaphone.

Vince looked up. "Go ahead," he replied.

Immediately, the rescue workers started to lower a stretcher down to us.

Vince again focused on Rubble.

"You were quite lucky," he said to me, "but I am not so sure about your dog." Then he thought for a moment. "Can you distract him? Pat his head or something?"

I did as he asked with my good arm. Just as Rubble seemed to relax a bit, Vince leaned over and gave him an injection right in his rump.

"That'll do it," Vince said.

We both watched Rubble slowly lower his head. Then his eyes began to flutter and his breathing slowed. A few seconds later, he was asleep.

That's when my transport arrived!

CHAPTER 11

RESCUED!

I was the first to get out of there.

The doctor put the stretcher on the uneven ground. He had me roll sideways while he slipped the stretcher in under me, then strapped me down.

They couldn't lift me horizontally—there just wasn't enough space in the cleared passage. So I was hauled upright and carried upwards like that—neck brace, hard hat, dust mask and all.

As I was slowly lifted towards the land of the living, I saw patches of blue sky. I realised from the light that it must be morning. The view reminded me how lucky I was to be alive. Twisted and broken debris—there was so much devastation everywhere. I don't know how I got out of there with as few injuries as I had.

Things really got eerie on my way up when I passed recognisable fragments of the Alexanders' milk bar. I saw a grubby, partially torn piece of paper that read:

**Lost dog.
Very friendly.**

I wondered how Rubble was going. He was now being tended by Vince.

From above, I heard a TV reporter announce, "The twelve-year-old boy we've all been watching for nearly sixteen hours is now being hauled up. From what we can tell, Jonathon has only minor injuries."

That announcement was quickly followed by another voice.

"Jonathon!" my mum screamed down. "Jonathon!"

I tried to look up as much as I could while dangling vertically, strapped to a stretcher. I managed a small smile.

"Mum!" I croaked.

Well, of course I was taken to hospital. The diagnosis—a fractured right arm and a cracked rib. Bruises on my back and legs and several cuts and gashes—some I didn't even know I had. The gash on my forehead was the only one that needed stitches.

Rubble was taken to an animal hospital and was in a serious condition.

They kept me in the hospital for three days. I wrote down most of this story while I was in bed.

I learned as I lay there that others hadn't been as lucky as I was. Over 200 people died from the earthquake, and hundreds of homes and buildings were damaged or destroyed. Our home—several kilometres away from the inner city—had broken windows, and we lost a lot of dishes, cups and glasses, but apart from that it was fine.

The earthquake's epicentre had been right on West Street. There is a fault—a fracture in the ground—in that area and it had shifted. The earthquake measured 7.1 on the Richter scale, which is considered to be dangerously high.

My time in the hospital not only included medical attention, but attention from well-wishers as well. Suddenly, friends and relatives I didn't even know were sending me cards, flowers and presents. I was on TV a few more times, too. I was famous—or nearly!

The day I left, my mum took me towards the hospital exit in a wheelchair. To my surprise (and relief), both Alexanders showed up for the occasion, too! Their injuries were mostly just cuts and bruises. They were both out the back of the shop attending to a delivery after the first trembler, which is probably what saved them once the big earthquake hit.

As Mum signed the hospital release papers, I squinted around me, looking at the sun-drenched world outside. I recognised our car, which was waiting out the front. Something familiar and normal!

Finally, Mum turned towards me. "Here we go," she announced.

"Wait a second," I said. "You haven't told me about Rubble. When does he get out?"

Mum paused and gathered her thoughts. I saw some of the answer on her face. "He has a broken leg and some other injuries," she said. "He's still in the animal hospital. He's been through a lot, and it's going to take time, but the vets think he will make it okay."

Mum wheeled me outside, but the bright day was blurred by my tears.

Once we got to the footpath, I stood up, gingerly, and hobbled over to the car.

Poor Rubble, I thought, as Mum opened the door.

I slid into the back seat and blurted out, "Can we visit Rubble in the hospital?"

"Sure," Mum replied. "I was hoping to do that as soon as you were ready."

"Well, that's right now," I said, without hesitation.

So I wasn't going home just yet!

And that's my story from four days in February 2009—at least as best I can remember.

Jonathon
